ALL YEAR LONG

NANCY TAFURI

GREENWILLOW BOOKS, NEW YORK

FOR MY FAMILY

writing from the Publisher,
Greenwillow Books,
a division of
William Morrow & Company, Inc.,
1350 Avenue of the Americas,
New York, NY 10019.
Printed in U.S.A.
First Edition
10 9 8 7 6 5 4 3 2

Library of Congress Cataloging in Publication Data
Tafuri, Nancy.   All year long.
Summary: Pictures a variety of activities on different
days of the week during each month of the year
from a Monday in January to a Saturday in December.
[1. Days—Fiction. 2. Months—Fiction] I. Title
PZ7.T117Al 1983   [E]   82-9275
ISBN 0-688-01414-3   AACR2
ISBN 0-688-01416-X (lib. bdg.)

Sunday

in JANUARY.

Monday

in FEBRUARY

and in
MARCH.

Tuesday

in APRIL

and in MAY.

Wednesday in JUNE

and in JULY!

Thursday

in AUGUST

and

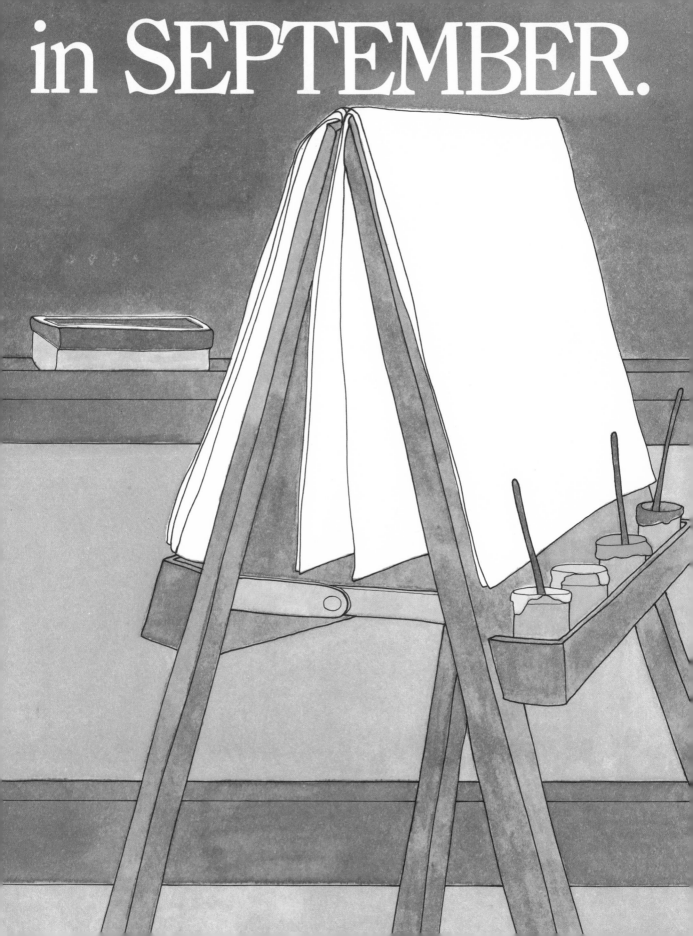

and

in NOVEMBER.

And Saturday in

DECEMBER.

ALL YEAR LONG
THE TWELVE MONTHS

1	JANUARY	JULY	7
2	FEBRUARY	AUGUST	8
3	MARCH	SEPTEMBER	9
4	APRIL	OCTOBER	10
5	MAY	NOVEMBER	11
6	JUNE	DECEMBER	12

E